DESTI N ATION
LOS ANGELES

Oregon

CANADA

UNITED STATES

MEXICO

N
W E
S

San Francisco

UNITED STATES

Nevada

California

PACIFIC OCEAN

SANTA MONICA MOUNTAINS

SAN GABRIEL MOUNTAINS

Los Angeles   Long Beach

San Nicholas

Santa Catalina

San Clemente

San Diego

Arizona

Baja California

MEXICO

Legend

⚓ Port City

| 0 | 35 | 70 miles |
| 0 | 35 | 70 kilometers |

DESTINATION
LOS ANGELES

by Dianne MacMillan

Lerner Publications Company • Minneapolis

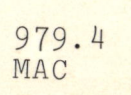

PHOTO ACKNOWLEDGMENTS

Cover photo by Chuck Place. All inside photos courtesy of Chuck Place, pp. 5, 12 (right), 16, 62, 64 (both), 66, 67, 70, 73 (both), 74; Port of Los Angeles, pp. 6, 9 (both), 13, 14, 18 (both), 21 (top and bottom), 22 (both), 24 (top), 27, 50 (both), 57 (left), 59, 60, 61, 75; Leon Callaway, pp. 12 (left), 15, 17, 21 (middle), 23, 24 (bottom), 25, 38, 40, 41, 42, 46, 48, 57 (right), 71; Shirley Jordan, p. 28; © Frank Balthis, p. 30; Bancroft Library, p. 31 (top); Corbis-Bettmann, pp. 31 (bottom), 35; courtesy of Banning Residence Museum, p. 33; Archive Photos/American Stock, p. 36; Archive Photos, pp. 37, 44; Mariners' Museum, Newport News, Virginia, p. 45; © T.R. Nichols, p. 51; Reuters/Corbis-Bettmann, p. 53; Courtesy of Korea National Tourism Corporation, p. 55; California Cartage Company, Inc., p. 56 (both); © James Blank/Root Resources, p. 68. Maps by Ortelius Design.

Website address: www.lernerbooks.com

LIBRARY OF CONGRESS CATALOGING-IN-PUBLICATION DATA

MacMillan, Dianne
    Destination Los Angeles / by Dianne MacMillan
      p. cm. — (Port cities of North America)
    Includes index.
    Summary: An introduction to the port city of Los Angeles describing its geology, history, economy, and day-to-day life.
    ISBN 0-8225-2786-3 (lib. bdg. : alk. paper)
    Los Angeles (Calif.)—Juvenile literature. [1. Los Angeles (Calif.)] I. Title. II. Series
    F869.L84M3 1997
    917.94'94—dc21   96-37407

Manufactured in the United States of America
1 2 3 4 5 6 – JR – 02 01 00 99 98 97

The glossary that begins on page 76 gives definitions of words shown in **bold type** in the text.

CONTENTS

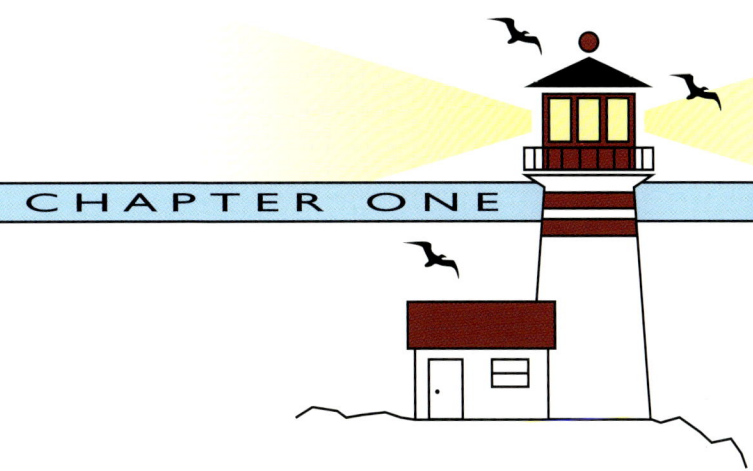

CHAPTER ONE

THE PORT ON THE PACIFIC

A seagull approaching the Port of Los Angeles would look down from its lofty view and see something that resembles a giant watery squid with its tentacles reaching inland. Every day ships make their way up and down the tentacle-like channels of this busy ocean port.

Location ➤ The Port of Los Angeles, or until 1997 WORLD-PORT LA, is located about 20 miles from downtown Los Angeles and is one of the busiest ports in the United States. The Santa Monica and San Gabriel Mountains rim the city on the east and north. The Pacific Ocean is on the port's western and southern boundaries.

Metropolitan Los Angeles sprawls over a large portion of southwestern California. The state is

The Port of Los Angeles (top of facing page) *stretches along California's Pacific coast, while the city of Los Angeles sprawls inland.*

bordered by Oregon to the north, Nevada and Arizona to the east, and Mexico to the south. Off the Los Angeles coast lie the islands of Santa Catalina, San Nicolas, San Clemente, and Santa Barbara.

Developers set up the bustling Port of Los Angeles at the mouth of the Los Angeles River, which empties into the Pacific Ocean at San Pedro Bay. Within this unprotected bay, rimmed with mudflats and marshes, builders created one of the world's largest artificial harbors.

The U.S. author Richard Henry Dana sailed into San Pedro Bay in 1835. In his book *Two Years before the Mast,* he wrote of the joy he felt when he saw his "last view of that place which was universally called the hell of California and seemed in every way designed for wear and tear on sailors." How surprised Dana might be to see this modern port, which encompasses 7,500 acres of land and sheltered water.

The port, which has grown rapidly since the 1940s, has 28 miles of waterfront with 28 terminals that handle cargo ranging from **containers** to automobiles and **bulk cargo.** Cruise passenger terminals, canneries, factories, boat slips, beaches, shops, and restaurants complete the variety offered by the Port of Los Angeles.

The Port of Los Angeles adjoins the Port of Long Beach, another large facility to the east. The Cerritos Channel links the two ports. Surrounding the entrances of the two ports is an extensive breakwater, built to provide a sheltered place for ships to safely anchor. The nine-mile-long breakwater, the largest in the world, is made from rectangular granite blocks weigh-

◀ **A Tour of the Port**

A breakwater (above) *protects San Pedro Bay from the harsh ocean waters. The light station at Angels Gate* (below) *greets ships entering and leaving the Port of Los Angeles through the breakwater.*

ing at least eight tons each. At low tide, the wall rises 14 feet above the surface of the water.

The breakwater begins on the western side of the harbor at Cabrillo Beach. Just west of Cabrillo, jutting out into the ocean on a high cliff, stands Point Fermin Lighthouse. The lighthouse—built in 1874—was once a much needed sentinel, warning sailors of the area's rocky outcrops and shallow waters. Although wartime blackouts caused the lighthouse's beam to be turned off during World War II (1939–1945), it remains a harbor landmark.

Ships approaching the port pass by a modern light station as they enter an opening in the breakwater called Angels Gate. The area just inside the breakwater is the Outer Harbor. Sailors call the Outer Harbor "Hurricane Gulch," because each day the winds blow hard for six hours between 11:00 A.M. and 5:00 P.M.

Los Angeles

WILMINGTON

Intermodal Container
Transfer Facility (ICTF)

Harry Bridges Boulevard

Alameda Corridor

Terminal Island Freeway

47

Cerritos Channel

Yang Ming Terminal

West Basin

Trans Pacific Container Corporation

East Basin

Terminal Island

GATX

110

Vincent Thomas Bridge

Turning Basin

47

Los Angeles Export Facility

World Cruise Center

Evergreen Container Terminal

Pier 300

SAN PEDRO

Pasha/Honda Automobile Terminal

Fish Harbor

Ports O' Call Village

SP Slip

American President Lines Container Terminal

West Channel/Cabrillo Beach Recreation Complex

Main Channel

Reservation Point

Pier 400 (Under Construction)

Cabrillo Marine Aquarium

Glenn Anderson Ship Channel

Outer Harbor

Angels Gate

Point Fermin Lighthouse

San Pedro Breakwater

Angels Gate Lighthouse

10

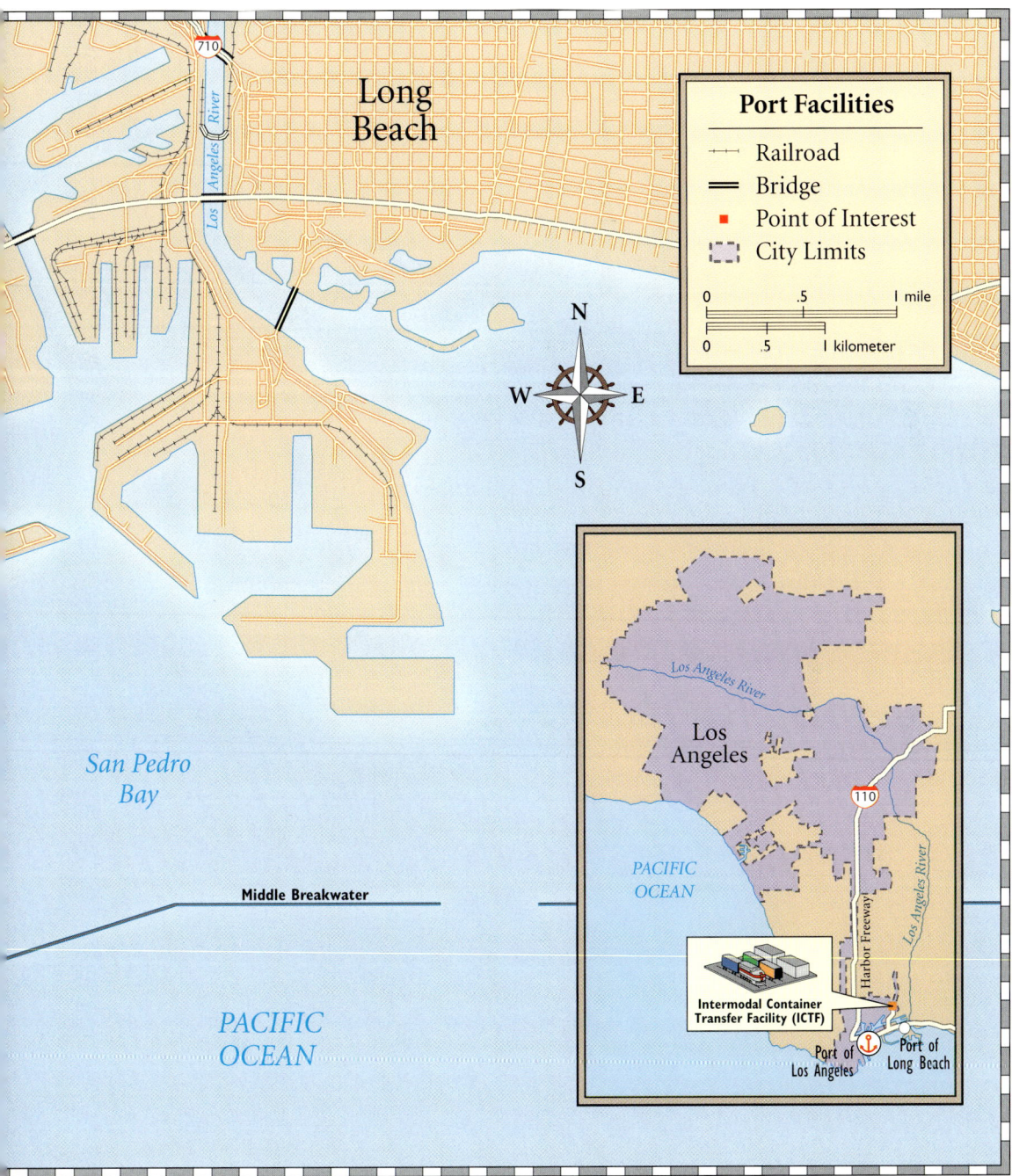

Long
Beach

Port Facilities

- ┼─┼ Railroad
- ═══ Bridge
- ■ Point of Interest
- ⌐ ¬ City Limits
  ⌐ ¬

```
0          .5        1 mile
0        .5      1 kilometer
```

N
W   E
S

San Pedro
Bay

Los Angeles River

Middle Breakwater

PACIFIC
OCEAN

Los
Angeles

Los Angeles River

110

Harbor Freeway

Los Angeles River

PACIFIC
OCEAN

Intermodal Container
Transfer Facility (ICTF)

Port of
Los Angeles

Port of
Long Beach

The shape of the port and its channels looks like a tree, with the Main Channel as the tree trunk and the smaller, connecting channels as branches. At the base of the tree is the vast Outer Harbor. Ships follow the Glenn Anderson Ship Channel—a central water route leading through the Outer Harbor—to the Main Channel. Several smaller waterways—West Channel, East Channel, and Fish Harbor—also branch out from the Outer Harbor to the left and right of the Main Channel.

The Main Channel and the smaller channels all are part of the Inner Harbor. Once inside the Inner Harbor, ships anchor at a wide variety of cargo terminals and passenger facilities. The West Channel/Cabrillo Beach Recreational Complex features a hotel, slips for 1,200 pleasure craft, Cabrillo Beach, shops, restaurants, and the Cabrillo Marine Aquarium. The East Channel is used primarily for loading and unloading bulk freight.

Two areas—Fish Harbor and the SP Slip, which lie on either side of the Main Channel—handle commercial fishing operations. To-

➤ Cabrillo Beach is one of the few recreational swimming beaches inside a heavily industrialized harbor.

Work crews (below left) *haul in their nets. Hundreds of fishing boats visit Fish Harbor and the SP Slip each day, making the Port of Los Angeles one of the nation's chief fishing ports. Rock cod* (below) *is a popular catch.*

Terminal Island houses several wharves in the port. Construction adds more wharves to the island's facilities.

gether these areas house 400,000 square feet of fish-processing facilities. The commercial fishing fleet in Los Angeles is the most productive on the West Coast of the United States, supplying most of the fresh fish available in California markets.

Ships proceeding up the Main Channel will see the Port Pilot's office on the left side of the Main Channel entrance. From this office, trained pilots travel past the breakwater to board most arriving ships and guide them safely through the harbor to the docks. The pilots also assist outgoing ships. The pilots' knowledge about local waters and weather conditions ensures that traffic will flow safely in and out of the port.

On the right side of the Main Channel entrance is Terminal Island. At the tip of the island, ships pass Reservation Point, which houses the U.S. Coast Guard and a federal prison. Shared by the Port of Los Angeles and the Port of Long Beach, Terminal Island began as a long, narrow strip of sand inhabited by reptiles. Over the years, tons of rock and mud have been dug out of the channels in the two ports to deepen the water level from 18 inches to 45 feet to accommodate larger ships. The land dug out during this **dredging** process was dumped onto Terminal Island to enlarge its land surface. Terminals, warehouses, and shipyards were then built on the hundreds of acres of newly created land.

Near the Coast Guard base are floating **dry docks** for ship repair. Also nearby are several terminals that handle liquid bulk products, including chemicals, petroleum, and crude oil. Two-thirds of California's oil fields and six major oil refineries are located within minutes of the port. Efficient transportation routes link the port to these oil fields and refineries, making oil exports and imports a mainstay of port operations since the early 1900s.

Proceeding up the Main Channel, ships pass the Municipal Fish Market and Ports O' Call Village. This area features shops, restaurants, and a maritime museum. Past the museum is the Pasha/Honda Automobile Terminal. One ship per week docks at this facility, and each ship carries from 2,000 to 5,000 automobiles imported from Asia.

Beyond the Pasha/Honda Automobile Terminal is the World Cruise Center, which serves nine cruise lines that together dock about 400

> ➤ Eighty shipping lines from more than 100 countries call at the Port of Los Angeles each year.

> ➤ Refined oil for gasoline and fuel, as well as more than 250 different types of petroleum-based chemicals, come from processed oil.

Eleven facilities at the port provide service for liquid bulk cargo, such as liquid petroleum. Storage tanks handle nearly 4 million tons of incoming and outgoing liquid petroleum products each year.

Wide-legged gantry cranes unload a container ship. The advent of containerization improved the speed and ease with which goods could move from ship to final destination.

ships each year. The ships annually bring more than 850,000 passengers to their vacation destinations. As many as five large cruise ships can dock at the center simultaneously.

Across the Main Channel on Terminal Island is the Evergreen Container Terminal. Its eight towering **gantry cranes** load and unload containers full of a wide variety of products. **Containerization** is the shipment of goods in weatherproof, secured, 20-foot-long metal containers that are sealed at the point of loading. The standard unit of measurement for container cargo is the 20-foot equivalent unit, or **TEU.** TEUs refer to the length of the container, not its weight. Most containers are 8.5 feet high by 8 feet deep by 20 feet long.

As ships continue through the Main Channel, they pass under the Vincent Thomas Bridge, which connects the mainland to Terminal Island. The four-lane toll bridge is the third longest suspension bridge in the United States, spanning 2.2 miles.

➤ Modern container ships can hold up to 6,000 TEUs.

➤ Modern tankers weigh up to 265,000 deadweight tons.

The area beyond the bridge is the Turning Basin, where ships can turn around to head back down the Main Channel or continue on to either the West Basin or the East Basin. Several large container terminals—GATX, Yang Ming, and Trans Pacific Container Corporation—stand along the docks of the West Basin. The East Basin leads to two other auto terminals and several other container terminals. Beyond the East Basin, the Cerritos Channel continues eastward into the adjacent Port of Long Beach.

The Vincent Thomas Bridge, one of the port's main landmarks, stretches for more than two miles. The bridge, which was completed in 1963, gives overland access to Terminal Island.

A number of facilities located in the Port of Los Angeles handle either dry or liquid bulk products. Several of these operations load and unload crude oil, petroleum products, chemicals, vegetable oils, and other liquid cargoes. Most of these terminals have storage facilities, and some use pipelines to move liquid products from the wharf to storage tanks.

◄ All Kinds of Cargo

Some bulk terminals handle dry bulk, including coal, petroleum coke, copper concentrates, and scrap metal. Exported items, such as petroleum coke, are unloaded onto a conveyor belt. Shiploaders can handle 1,400 tons of coal an hour, filling huge freighters. Imports unloaded by gantry cranes or clamshell buckets are stockpiled or directly loaded onto trucks or railroad **hopper cars.** Scrap metal from throughout southern California can be processed by an onsite shredder. A bulkloader dumps the scrap onto vessels for export.

Some products, such as oversized beams and pipes, large machinery, and autos, don't fit into containers and must go out as individual cargo items. Other products come in packaging materials that don't require the protection containers provide. These goods may be packaged in boxes, bags, or slings. Cut lumber is shipped on wrapped pallets. This type of packaged, noncontainerized cargo is called **breakbulk cargo.**

➤ The Vincent Thomas Bridge is referred to as the Green Giant, because of its green paint. A crew of transportation workers continuously paints the bridge. When they reach one end they start over again at the other end.

➤ GATX has five different terminals within the port.

Nearly indestructible bags—an example of breakbulk cargo—are loaded onto pallets and then moved onboard a ship for export.

The Port of Los Angeles is a major distribution point for the import and export of autos, trucks, and vans. Three separate facilities handle and store several brands of automobiles. Automobiles are one of the port's leading import cargoes. In fact, more than 350,000 cars come through the port each year, mainly from Asia. Workers load the vehicles onto trucks for shipment to auto dealers throughout the United States.

From the earliest days of commercial operations, the Port of Los Angeles has had lumber, petroleum, boatbuilding, fishing, and canning facilities. But during the 1960s, the advent of containers revolutionized shipping. Shippers send products such as clothing, toys, footwear, and electronics equipment in containers. The Port of Los Angeles also has begun handling new reefer containers from Australia and New Zealand. These larger containers have refrigeration units and can haul any perishable com-

Automobiles (above), *among the port's main cargo items, leave the port from one of three terminals devoted solely to the shipment of cars. Container facilities have started implementing refrigeration units to handle perishable items such as bananas* (left).

modity from frozen meats to chilled fruits and vegetables. Containerization has reduced the amount of labor needed, has cut loading and unloading time dramatically, and has simplified storage.

The Port of Los Angeles has six container terminals that offer more than 576 acres of container handling facilities and 38 gantry cranes for moving containers. Crane operators sit in 200-foot-high cabins, from which they lower huge prongs called spreaders that lift containers on or off ships. The cranes are able to load or unload 30 containers an hour. More than 2 million containers move through the Port of Los Angeles each year, making it one of the busiest container ports in the United States.

Intermodal Transport and Port Connections > Moving commodities in the same closed container unit using two or more different modes of transport is known as **intermodal transport.** Ships bring containers full of various import cargoes, for example, across the ocean to the port where crews and equipment load the cargo containers directly onto trucks. The trucks carry the containers to railroad connections or across the country to their final destination. The 114-acre Intermodal Container Transfer Facility (ICTF) takes care of most of these transfers. Opened in 1986, the ICTF is located four miles northeast of the port area. At the ICTF, containers leaving the port by truck are transferred to trains to be transported to points across the country. Meanwhile, containers arriving by train from other parts of the country are moved onto trucks and hauled to the port.

Trucks that are ready to load up at the ICTF drive through the truck gate in 1 of 16 lanes. Each truck is loaded with containers. Workers can process as many as 230 containers per hour. The ICTF relies on computerized tracking of containers, a control tower to oversee the traffic, and an on-site U.S. Customs office to inspect import cargoes.

Freight trains equipped with doublestack rail cars move directly into the ICTF on six rail tracks. Equipment stacks two containers on each flat railcar bed. Approximately 80 doublestack trains depart each week for key points throughout the United States. The ICTF can handle up to 500,000 containers per year and can be equipped to handle even higher volumes. Port officials are also developing plans for new facilities on Terminal Island.

Railroad tracks encircle the Port of Los Angeles, and some warehouses and container terminals have direct rail connections to the tracks. Three transcontinental railroads—the Southern Pacific Transportation Company, the Union Pacific Railroad Company, and the Burlington Northern Santa Fe Railway Company—link the port to destinations across the Americas.

The port is also served by the Harbor Belt Line Railroad, which is owned jointly by the three transcontinental railroads and the port. This railroad system is used for cargo distribution and switching (moving cars from one track to another) in the immediate harbor area.

About 70 separate trucking companies service the port. Three freeways link the port to three major interstate highways, providing direct access to the United States, Mexico, and Canada.

The Intermodal Container Transfer Facility (ICTF) (right) *is integral to Los Angeles's success as a container port. Containers arrive via ship* (below) *and are transferred to trucks, which take them to the ICTF. At the transfer facility, cranes stack containers by twos onto railcars* (bottom), *which then deliver the goods to destinations throughout the United States.*

The port is also near the Los Angeles International Airport, the nation's second busiest cargo airport.

A visitor crossing the Vincent Thomas Bridge is ◄ **Building for the Future**
likely to see several construction projects taking place on Terminal Island. Crews are building several new terminals and are realigning roads to accommodate the construction. The projects are part of the Port of Los Angeles's $600 million construction program called Pier 300/400 Implementation. The long-term construction plan encompasses 24 separate projects. Many of the projects were designed to address the ongoing growth in trade with Pacific Rim nations (countries that border the Pacific Ocean).

The construction program includes 10 new terminals, 5,000 feet of new deepwater berths, 5 new highways, 35 miles of new railroad track,

Pier 400 (facing page, left) *is taking shape. Much of the pier's landfill comes from dredging the harbor* (facing page, right), *an improvement that will also deepen the harbor to accommodate ever-larger ships. Pier 400 will add 582 acres of useable terminal space to the port. Construction crews build railroad tracks* (above) *for the new American President Lines terminal that opened in 1997 on Pier 300.*

a new Terminal Island Container Transfer Facility, and the largest dredging and reclamation project in U.S. history. The dredging produces water depths of 45 to 63 feet within the port channels. The deeper waters accommodate larger container and dry-bulk ships, which continue to increase in size and weight.

Dredging has produced the landfill for a new section—Pier 300—added on to Terminal Island. A shipping company, American President Lines, has moved onto this new property. When construction is fully complete, Terminal Island will be the largest artificial island in the world. Landfill is also being used to create another facility—Pier 400—in the Outer Harbor.

Another part of the expansion program is a 20-mile, 6-lane commercial highway and rail system called the Alameda Corridor. The corridor will provide a safe, high-speed link between the port and downtown Los Angeles. From this point, freight trains can hook up easily with the transcontinental railroad network and trucks can quickly access the interstate highway system.

The port is dedicated to preserving as many local habitats as possible. A kelp transplantation program in the late 1970s relocated giant kelp from Mexico's Baja Peninsula to the breakwater in Los Angeles Harbor. The kelp provides a habitat for a wide variety of fish.

◀ Environmental Issues

The rapid growth of the port since the 1940s has affected the marine life of the surrounding marshy tidelands. Dockside industries have dumped harmful pollutants into the harbor over the years.

Fighting pollution became a top priority of the Los Angeles Harbor Department in 1969. At that time, the Harbor Commission, which runs the port, adopted a policy to end toxic dumping. The commission pressured the shipping industry and local governments to work harder to rid the port of pollution. Tenants and users of the harbor complied with the new policies. Within a year, the water in the harbor cleared dramatically. Fish, pelicans, and sea lions returned.

Three years later, the Harbor Commission established the Environmental Management Office—the first environmental office at any U.S.

Pelicans (right) *and sea lions* (facing page) *have also returned to the area.*

port. The Environmental Management Office is staffed by scientists who routinely monitor the wildlife and the water and air quality of the Port of Los Angeles and the southern California coastal area.

Scientists analyze water samples from every part of the Los Angeles Harbor at least once a month. In the Outer Harbor, the Environmental Management Office also is establishing shallow-water habitats where fish can breed and birds can nest. The Port of Los Angeles is considered one of the cleanest harbors in the world. Protecting the natural environment of the port as it continues to expand and grow will help ensure the future of a healthy port.

SAVING THE LEAST TERN

The California least tern is a small waterfowl that nests in sandy areas along lagoons and estuaries (points where rivers and oceans meet). Recognized as an endangered species by both federal authorities and the state of California, the least tern populates parts of the coast from San Francisco to the Mexican border. Working with local, state, and federal agencies, the Port of Los Angeles has played a major role in implementing projects designed to save the terns by saving the habitat where they lay their eggs.

Each year the harbor maintains 15 acres of sandy marsh area as a nesting site for the terns. Because of development within the harbor, the nesting site is moved annually, but the amount of land reserved for the birds remains constant. In 1996 the port created a 190-acre shallow-water habitat in the Outer Harbor. The habitat shelters juvenile fish and is a feeding ground for the terns.

In a much larger project, the Port of Los Angeles is spending approximately $55 million dollars to revitalize the Batiquitos Lagoon in northern San Diego County. Shut off from tidal water because of heavy development, the lagoon was filling with sediment and was no longer attracting shorebirds. In 1995 a 1.5-acre nesting site at the lagoon drew 72 pairs of least terns. The following year, observers saw 132 nesting pairs. When the restoration is finished, Batiquitos Lagoon will have more than 30 acres of newly created habitat for the endangered birds and other wildlife.

Environmental projects earn the Port of Los Angeles **mitigation credits,** which it can use to legally expand landfill areas in the harbor. In addition, improving the environment of California's coast enhances the quality of life for everyone—not just the least terns.

The Port of Los Angeles has made an effort to protect the sandy areas where least terns are known to lay their eggs.

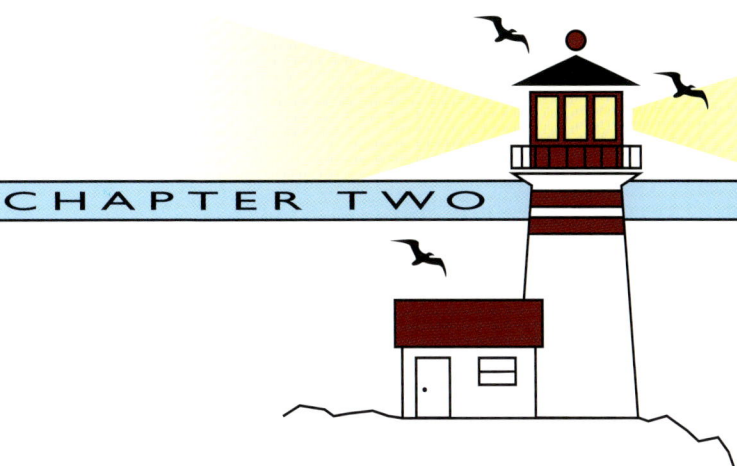

CHAPTER TWO

SAN PEDRO BAY

Thousands of years ago, a Native American people called the Tongva lived in the area that is present-day Los Angeles. The land was a natural wilderness covered with oak trees and low brush. Mudflats and swamps lined the coast. The Tongva hunted small game; gathered acorns, berries, wild oats, and seaweed; and speared fresh fish and sea creatures from the ocean.

Tongva people built lightweight canoes known as *ti'ats* by lashing together thin pieces of pine planks. The ti'ats were sometimes 30 feet long. Two people could easily carry a canoe to the mudflats and marshy tidelands. The

Before Europeans arrived in California, Native Americans fished, hunted, and lived off the land; practiced their own religions; and spoke their own languages. Activities at Mission San Gabriel Arcángel (facing page) *changed life for the Indians forever.*

water in this area was seldom deeper than 18 inches at low tide. The Tongva hunters paddled out a mile or more to deeper water to spear large fish and sea mammals.

The Tongva also lived on the nearby islands of Santa Catalina, San Nicolas, San Clemente, and Santa Barbara. These people mined a soft rock called steatite, or soapstone, and made bowls, pans, pipes, beads, and carvings from the rock. Other Native American groups in the region wanted steatite. The Tongva began to trade with these neighboring groups, exchanging steatite for deerskins and other goods.

The first European to sail by the swampy  **Newcomers Arrive** coastal marshlands of what became the Port of Los Angeles was the Portuguese explorer, Juan Rodriguez Cabrillo. In 1542 he saw the crescent-shaped mudflats and wrote in his log, "The bay . . . is an excellent harbor and the country is good with many plains and groves

Juan Rodriguez Cabrillo first laid eyes on the southern coast of California in 1542 near what eventually would become Los Angeles.

Smoke poured from Tongva sweat lodges (above). *More Europeans came to the area after Cabrillo, mostly from Spain. The Tongva, curious about the newcomers, gathered to watch the religious ceremonies* (below) *performed by Spanish priests.*

of trees." Cabrillo saw smoke rising from Tongva fires and named the shallow inlet Bahia de los Fumos, or Bay of Smokes. The bay was called by different names until 1734, when a Spaniard named the inlet San Pedro Bay.

The tranquility of the area changed with the arrival of Spanish missionaries, who came to bring the Indian people under the rule of the Spanish king, to convert the Indians to the Catholic religion, and to teach them Spanish customs. The mission San Gabriel Arcángel was founded in 1771, 40 miles inland from San Pedro Bay. Five years later, San Juan Capistrano, to the south, became the sixth mission in California.

The missionaries at San Gabriel and San Juan Capistrano began to trade at San Pedro Bay, hauling oxcarts loaded with animal hides and tallow (animal fat used in making candles and soap) to the edge of the little harbor. Twice a year, supply ships arrived from Spain. Crews loaded the hides and tallow onto the ships in exchange for supplies—such as coffee beans, chocolate, blankets, and metal utensils and tools.

The mission trade also encouraged other settlements. In 1781 eleven families from the Spanish colony of New Spain (present-day Mexico) founded El Pueblo de Nuestra Señora la Reina de Los Angeles, or The Town of Our Lady the Queen of Angels. Before these settlers arrived, the site had been the Tongva village Yang-na. No one could have guessed that the small town eventually would grow into a city with more than 3.5 million people.

New Spain gained its independence in 1821, becoming the nation of Mexico. In the 1820s, Mexico took control of California and expanded trade. San Pedro Bay quickly became one of the largest and busiest hide-trading centers on the Pacific Coast. But getting goods to and from the port was hard work. The bay was still mostly swamps and tidal flats. A long, narrow island, called Rattlesnake Island, blocked all but a narrow opening to the ocean.

South of Rattlesnake Island rose Deadman's Island, a rocky outcropping close to shore. Between Deadman's Island and the mainland lay a long bar of sand and rocks. The water depth over the sandbar was only 18 inches. Because the water was so shallow, ship captains had no choice but to anchor offshore and then move goods through the shallow water in small boats called lighters. The slow, difficult work was one of the reasons Richard Henry Dana was so disenchanted with San Pedro on his 1835 voyage.

In spite of the challenges, brokers (merchants) in Boston, Massachusetts, sent more and more trading ships to the area after California became a territory of the United States in 1848. The traders purchased leather hides for the fast-growing shoe industry in New England. Hides brought in $2.00 apiece. At San Pedro Bay, men threw the hides over the cliffs to sailors waiting on the beach below. The sailors balanced the hides on their heads and waded out to the lighters, which carried the hides to the ships anchored outside the bay. When a ship was loaded with as many as 40,000 hides, it set sail. Despite the bay's distance from Los Angeles, its lack of a calm, natural harbor, and its lack of convenient docking facilities, the bay area became a major trading site.

Development of the Port ➤ The growth of Los Angeles and its port resulted from the work of a few determined citizens. One of the first to see the port's potential was Diego Sepulveda. Sepulveda was an heir to Rancho Los Palos Verdes, a property that included all of San Pedro Bay, the high bluffs, and surrounding flatland. In 1849 Sepulveda began a stagecoach line to carry passengers and cargo between the bay and the growing town of Los Angeles. On the cliffs, he installed a shelter for waiting passengers and a storehouse. On the beach below, Sepulveda built Sepulveda's Landing—the first primitive wharf on San Pedro Bay.

After gold was discovered in California in 1848, thousands of new entrepreneurs came looking for riches. In 1851, a year after California became a state, Phineas Banning arrived in Los Angeles. He was only 21 and penniless, but

Phineas Banning

33

he immediately saw the potential of the harbor. Banning rented a boat and sold kegs of fresh water to ships anchored beyond the bay. Then he hired on as a stagecoach driver with the Temple & Alexander Shipping firm.

Within a year, Banning bought his employer's stagecoach line and began to compete with the Sepulveda stage line. Five years later, Banning had more than 15 passenger coaches and 50 wagons for freight. His stagecoaches carried freight for the U.S. government from the harbor at San Pedro to military outposts in California, New Mexico, Utah, Arizona, and Texas.

Banning faced stiff competition for business. In 1857, after a storm destroyed the San Pedro wharf, he moved his business to a new location five miles to the northeast. He bought 2,400 acres of waterfront property, dug out a channel, and built his own wharf. Banning called his site New San Pedro, later renaming it Wilmington. Because the water at the new wharf was still very shallow, Banning built a fleet of flat-bottomed barges and shallow steamers to carry passengers and freight to waiting ships outside the bay.

As southern California's population grew, settlers needed lumber to build homes. Although the warm climate produced lots of vegetation, the area didn't have many trees. Lumber harvested in other areas quickly became a leading import in Los Angeles. In turn, Californians grew citrus fruits and other warm-weather crops. These commodities were exported to places with short growing seasons. Expanded trade helped create new jobs and enabled the people of the Los Angeles area to prosper.

➤ Phineas Banning eventually earned the name Father of Los Angeles Harbor.

A traction engine, developed in the 1800s, helped to improve the efficiency of logging to meet the increasing demand for lumber in the Los Angeles area.

Banning handled most of the trade in hides, tallow, grapes, oranges, whale and shark oil, lumber, and wire until the early 1860s.

Railroads and the Free Harbor Fight ▶ In November 1865, voters elected Banning to the California State Senate. He then introduced the first railroad bill to the state legislature. The bill passed, and in 1869 the Los Angeles & San Pedro Railroad began service between San Pedro Bay and Los Angeles. This 21-mile stretch of track was the first railroad in southern California. Even though the railroad was named for San Pedro, the track ended in Wilmington at Banning's dock, because Banning was one of the railroad company's owners. Rail service—which eventually connected California with the rest of the United States—marked the beginning of a new era of development for the harbor region. Rail service also began a 30-year struggle, known as the Free Harbor Fight.

Railroads provided a vital link for transporting cargo between the harbor and the growing city. Whoever controlled the railroad controlled harbor activity. The Southern Pacific Railroad, owned by Collis P. Huntington,

moved into southern California in 1876 and began competing with the Los Angeles & San Pedro Railroad.

Within a few years, Southern Pacific dominated rail traffic in the area and began charging enormous fees. In fact, it cost more to move goods from San Pedro Bay to Los Angeles than it did to ship them across the Pacific Ocean from San Pedro to Hong Kong in Asia. The people of Los Angeles were angry. They felt the harbor should not be under the thumb of only one person or business. The public demanded change, but Huntington had powerful friends in government and was allowed to maintain control over rail traffic in Los Angeles.

In the late 1800s, thousands of tons of lumber and coal were moving through San Pedro and Wilmington. Other industries also began to operate in the harbor. A San Francisco firm established the California Fish Company, the first cannery in Los Angeles Harbor, followed

Passengers arrive from St. Louis on the Southern Pacific Railroad in 1885. Railroads helped connect the Port of Los Angeles with the rest of the nation.

later by Van Camp Sea Food and French Sardine Company. With railroad connections to the rest of the country, the Port of Los Angeles became the leading commercial fishing center in the United States.

Rugged deep-sea fishermen pose for a picture on a ship's deck. Local canneries made it possible to preserve fish for longer amounts of time and to ship saltwater catches inland to landlocked states.

Other railroad owners wanted a part of the growing trade business and decided to create their own ports on the coast to get around the Huntington monopoly. The Atchison Topeka & Santa Fe Railroad built a track line from Los Angeles to present-day Marina del Rey with the intention of establishing a seaport. Then the Redondo Railway Company laid tracks from Los Angeles to Redondo and installed a wharf there.

In 1885 a company in St. Louis, Missouri, bought Rattlesnake Island and renamed it

Terminal Island. The company installed a railroad line that ran from Los Angeles down to the San Pedro shoreline, where the developers set up a terminal. Meanwhile, Phineas Banning led a crusade to solicit the U.S. Congress for money to improve San Pedro's harbor. Banning understood that the port could not continue to grow unless the channels were dredged and a breakwater was built. These improvements would allow ships to berth at the harbor facilities rather than anchor offshore.

Collis Huntington had other plans, however. He wanted to build another port at Santa Monica, a small town a few miles up the coast. Huntington owned most of the oceanfront. He planned for his railroad to completely bypass San Pedro and Wilmington and to carry all passengers and cargo from Los Angeles to Santa Monica Bay. With the allotted harbor funds going to his port instead of to San Pedro, Hunt-

Terminal Island (formerly known as Rattlesnake Island) added useful space to the Port of Los Angeles. The island got its name because it was the end of the line for the railroads.

ington would have a monopoly over all shipping commerce in southern California.

In 1894 Huntington told the people of Los Angeles, "I do not find it to my advantage to have a harbor built at San Pedro and I shall be compelled to oppose all efforts that you make to secure appropriations for that site." The battle lines were drawn. For five years, Huntington and the people of Los Angeles waged a legal battle over which site should receive money to construct a deepwater harbor.

Huntington was so sure that the U.S. Congress would choose his site that he ordered construction of the longest wooden pier in the world in Santa Monica. Almost a mile long, it was called the Long Wharf. Ocean vessels immediately began anchoring at the convenient Long Wharf, taking business away from San Pedro. It looked like Huntington's plans would succeed. But he met opposition from an unlikely source.

California Senator Stephen M. White favored San Pedro as the main port in southern California. Senator White skillfully argued for two days before the U.S. Senate in 1886, making a case for funding a port at San Pedro. White also added an amendment to the bill, requiring that a board of engineers—not the U.S. Congress—choose the site of the port. Furthermore, the Southern Pacific Railroad would be forced to allow other railroads to use its tracks at a reasonable price.

The amended bill passed and became law in 1896. One year later, the board of engineers decided in favor of San Pedro. Huntington's friends in Congress worked hard to prevent the appropriations from being awarded. It took two more years and action by U.S. president William McKinley before the funds were awarded and improvements began. The Free Harbor Fight was over, and Senator White was hailed as San Pedro's savior. A bronze statue in his honor was erected in downtown Los Angeles. (The statue still stands near the port, on Stephen White Street at the entrance to Cabrillo Beach.)

By the turn of the century, Los Angeles had ◀ **The Port in the 1900s**
grown to a population of 100,000 people. The city began annexing surrounding communities like a hungry shark. Because Los Angeles had access to a freshwater pipeline that carried water from northern California, many smaller communities joined the city willingly. In 1907 Los Angeles annexed a strip of land 1 mile wide and 16 miles long between the city's southern border and the outskirts of San Pedro and Wilmington. Two years later, the communities of San Pedro and Wilmington became part of Los Angeles. Thus the bay—with harbor facilities at San Pedro and Wilmington—officially became the Port of Los Angeles.

In the early 1900s, a train hauled rocks from nearby quarries to use in constructing the breakwater.

The city of Los Angeles created a harbor commission to oversee all port activities and development. Construction began on an 8,500-foot section of a new breakwater. The Main Channel was also widened to 800 feet and dredged to a depth of 30 feet. At the same time, the Southern Pacific Railroad completed its first major wharf, where railcars could load and unload goods simultaneously.

The timing of these improvements was perfect. On August 15, 1914, the Panama Canal in

In a spray of salt water, another rock was added to what would become a nine-mile-long breakwater.

Central America opened for business. Ships carrying cargo from Atlantic Ocean ports could pass through the new canal to get to the Pacific Ocean. Prior to the opening of the Panama Canal, ships traveling from the Atlantic to the Pacific had to sail thousands of miles around the tip of South America.

The Port of Los Angeles had a unique advantage over other West Coast ports. It lay close to the Great Circle Route—a well-traveled sea route between the Panama Canal and Asia. For this reason, Los Angeles Harbor was to become a natural port of call for most trans-Pacific and coastal vessels.

Growth of the Port The port's greatest expansion of facilities took place during the 1920s. Many major waterfront installations built then are still in use. The linear footage of wharves doubled between 1921 and 1925. As a result of these improvements, more shipping lines began to use the port. The volume of petroleum, lumber, and citrus that was handled at the port increased, and the Port of Los Angeles surpassed San Francisco as the busiest seaport on the West Coast. Los Angeles ranked second only to New York in foreign tonnage.

Beginning in 1927, two years of steady blasting removed Deadman's Island. The tons of rock and debris were dumped on Terminal Island, adding 62 acres of landfill to create Reservation Point, where a few years later, a federal prison was built.

Although business and construction projects slowed during the Great Depression of the 1930s, an additional section of the breakwater and a few more passenger and cargo terminals were built. Competition for tenants and West Coast shipping lines came with the founding of Long Beach Harbor in 1931. The competition sparked a friendly but intense rivalry that encouraged the Port of Los Angeles to maintain and upgrade its facilities.

➤ In 1928 the port handled 26.5 million tons of cargo, more than any other U.S. port. This record stood for 40 years.

Deadman's Island (behind ship) *diminished in size in 1927 and 1928 due to blasting that crumbled the land. Terminal Island grew as a result.*

BLOODY THURSDAY

In the early 1930s, longshoremen and stevedores felt they were being mistreated by their employers because of corrupt hiring practices, low wages, and unsafe working conditions. Stevedores handled the cargo aboard ship, coming and going with the vessels. Longshoremen were based in port and moved cargo on the docks. The dissatisfied laborers organized into labor unions so they could bargain for better wages and working conditions.

Company owners and other antilabor groups actively discouraged union membership. On one occasion, an antiunion group attacked a union meeting. Union members were beaten, and seven of them were abducted to the nearby Santa Ana Mountains, where they were tarred and feathered. Conditions worsened in 1932, when workers took a 10-cent pay cut. In May of 1934, 1,300 disgruntled members of the International Longshoremen Association (ILA) walked off the job.

Lumber and shipping companies were not about to allow cargoes to sit on the docks and in idled ships. The companies hired 1,200 replacement workers (the union members called them scabs). The replacement workers were housed in circus tents built on the Wilmington waterfront. Company owners asked the police to patrol the tent city. In addition, the owners hired private security guards to back up the police.

The anger of union members focused on the tent city. On May 15, 1934, known as Bloody Thursday, striking union members set fire to the tents. Fists and clubs swung. Police and guards fired into the crowd. Two men were killed, and five others were seriously wounded. Dozens on both sides were beaten. Finally order was restored, and fireboats put out the tent fires. The strike lasted until July 26, 1934, when owners and workers reached a wage settlement. But Bloody Thursday would be remembered for many years to come.

A worker paints the finishing touches on a ship's stern. During World War II (1939–1945), shipbuilding was a major contributor to the Los Angeles economy, and also supplied the war effort with battleships.

The United States entered World War II after Japan bombed Pearl Harbor on December 7, 1941. Every boat and shipbuilding company at the Port of Los Angeles offered its services in construction, conversion, or repair of watercraft for the war effort. The California Shipbuilding Corporation (Calship) was the biggest shipbuilder, operating on 175 acres of semitidal lands on Terminal Island. Before the war, crews built about 6 ships each month. By the end of the war in 1945, the company was producing more than 20 battleships per month.

Other firms added to the quotas. Smaller companies, for example, manufactured patrol boats and landing craft. Still other companies repaired existing boats and returned them to

➤ Many of the ships destroyed or damaged in the attack on Pearl Harbor had regularly berthed at the Los Angeles Harbor. Many family members of the sailors stationed at Pearl Harbor lived in the community.

service at a rate of two per day. By the war's end, workers had launched a total of 559 ships from the San Pedro shipyards. During peak construction, wartime shipbuilding employed 90,000 laborers. Calship alone employed 55,000 workers.

Growth and Modernization ➤ After the war, crews finished the final leg of the breakwater, on the Long Beach side. Many returning soldiers and sailors decided to make their homes in warm California. This sparked a sharp increase in lumber imports for building homes.

An early attempt to streamline the process of loading, unloading, and distributing cargo was to pack products into railcars. The cars were then secured to the decks of barges, ready to roll after reaching their destination. Containerization further simplified the process.

The Port of Los Angeles shifted its attention from shipbuilding to other industries. The port began a publicity campaign to attract new customers by placing port information in more than 3,000 foreign and daily newspapers. As a result, some global companies expanded their shipping routes to include the Port of Los Angeles. In 1951 maritime trade resumed with Japan—a wartime enemy—after having stopped completely during the conflict. By 1952 Japanese merchant ships were regularly visiting the harbor. Four years later, in 1956, Japan led all other foreign countries in trade with Los Angeles, with 324 Japanese vessels sailing into the port. Many of the ships carried Japanese-made automobiles, which became one of the most valuable import products passing through the port.

Container cargo revolutionized the shipping industry. Matson Navigation Company is credited with sending the first containerized shipment from the Port of Los Angeles. The company shipped 20 containers aboard the

Hawaiian Merchant in August 1958. By the end of the year, the port had handled 7,000 containers.

Port authorities made a variety of changes to accommodate container cargo. Crews constructed stronger wharves that could support the additional weight of container cargo. Gantry cranes for loading and unloading containers were installed on the wharves. The Vincent Thomas Bridge opened to link the mainland to Terminal Island.

The new container ships—with deeper and wider hulls to fit the large, rectangular containers—needed deeper channels to navigate. So once again, the channel was dredged. At the same time, workers completed the world's largest underwater pipeline, extending from docked supertankers (extra-large crude oil tankers) to the General Petroleum facility on Terminal Island.

> ➤ In April 1959, Los Angeles voters approved an amendment allowing the harbor to finance $50 million dollars in bonds for improvements. The funds would be critical to future development.
>
> ➤ The Vincent Thomas Bridge opened to traffic in 1963, connecting Terminal Island to the mainland.

In 1963 the last section of the Vincent Thomas Bridge went into place.

> During 1971 and 1972, a longshoremen's strike stopped most of the work at the port. The strike lasted 135 days and drastically cut the amount of cargo handled.

> In 1995 about 726,000 travelers passed through the World Cruise Center at the Port of Los Angeles, making it the busiest passenger facility on the West Coast.

All of these changes helped the port adapt to new ways of shipping goods. Many of the older industries, such as fishing, boatbuilding, and lumber began to decline, however. To increase revenue at the port, developers added restaurants, shops, and cruise passenger terminals to the port's facilities.

In the mid-1970s, the port welcomed new tenants from Pacific Rim countries, such as the Taiwan-based shipping company Evergreen Line. As trade with Asia continued to increase, the port received financial assistance from the U.S. government. Engineers deepened the Main Channel to 45 feet so that the Port of Los Angeles could accommodate large oceangoing vessels.

During the 1980s, trucks and trains carried more and more goods between the Port of Los Angeles and cities throughout the country. The opening of the Intermodal Container Transfer Facility in 1986 made the loading and unloading of containerized cargo more efficient and more economical. In the first year of ICTF's operation, the port handled one million TEUs.

The Future of the Port ➤ By 1990 container movement through the Port of Los Angeles exceeded two million TEUs per year. This figure increased through the 1990s as containerized transport continued to grow. But as traffic at the port increases and as shipping companies utilize even larger vessels, the port has had to make plans to accommodate the growth. These plans include the ongoing development of the Pier 300/400 Implementation Program. The port is poised for increased growth and expansion as it readies itself for the next century.

CHAPTER THREE

THE PORT AT WORK

Tugboat operators keep their vessels in top condition, ready for towing ships within the port.

The primary business of any port is the import and export of goods and materials. Each area of the world has certain resources, food products, and manufactured goods, some of which the people there don't need. Likewise there are always other resources and products that are not available at home. By means of trade—the buying and selling of commodities—consumers are able to acquire a variety of products and to sell surplus goods. The demand for products creates more jobs as manufacturers increase the production of trade goods.

Imports and Exports ➤ In the mid-1990s, the Port of Los Angeles ranked first in the United States for the dollar amount of cargo handled at the port. In 1994

49

the cargo passing through the port was valued at $73.4 billion. The major trading partners of the Port of Los Angeles are Japan, South Korea, Taiwan, China, and Ecuador. Trade between Los Angeles and Japan alone accounted for $23.5 billion in 1996.

The Port of Los Angeles is a major distribution center for imports coming to the continent of North America. After arriving at the port, imported containers are transported by sea, rail, air, and road to all parts of the United States, Mexico, and Canada. The top five imports coming into the Port of Los Angeles are iron and steel shapes (slabs, beams, pipes, tubing, and coils used in construction), petroleum oils (gasoline and jet fuel), crude petroleum, bananas and plantains, and motor-vehicle parts. Most of the iron and steel shapes come from Brazil, and the petroleum oils arrive from Saudi Arabia. Venezuela sends its crude petroleum to the port, while the bananas and plantains come from Ecuador. Furniture arrives from China. In 1994 the port imported 1.2 million tons of iron

Petroleum (left, in storage tanks) *and steel pipes* (above) *are some of the most common goods that enter the Port of Los Angeles.*

Cranes pile up scrap metal to get it ready for shipping.

and steel shapes; 942,000 tons of petroleum oils; 823,000 tons of crude petroleum; 603,000 tons of bananas and plantains; and 2.4 million tons of furniture.

The top five exports moving through the port are coal (to Japan), petroleum coke (to Japan), petroleum oils (to China), wastepaper (to South Korea), and iron and steel scrap (to South Korea). In 1995 more than 1.8 million tons of coal were exported through the Port of Los Angeles. Petroleum coke and petroleum oils each accounted for 1.1 million tons. Tonnage for wastepaper was 780,000 tons, and the amount of iron and steel scrap exported was 747,000 tons.

Some of these exports are waste products from U.S. industries. Iron and steel scrap includes demolished cars, refrigerators, and other metal products. Foreign countries melt down the scrap to create metal for new products. Wastepaper is exported to Taiwan, Japan, and South Korea. Manufacturers there recycle the paper to make new paper products and building materials.

If two countries import and export the same dollar amount of goods, the countries have a trade balance. But if one country imports more products than it exports, the country is maintaining a trade deficit. In other words, more money is leaving the country to pay for foreign goods than is coming in from the sale of exports.

Imported products often cost less than do the same products manufactured domestically. Consumers naturally prefer to buy the less expensive goods. The result is lower demand for domestic products and less profit for domestic factories. The factories may have to lay off workers or close down their plants.

To keep industries from closing or laying off workers, governments may impose taxes called tariffs on imported foreign goods. Or they may not allow the foreign product into the country at all. Sometimes governments restrict imports by setting quotas, or limits, on how much of a specific product can be imported. Governments may also assist domestic manufacturers by offering monetary benefits called subsidies, which reduce production costs and allow for competitive pricing.

Countries faced with trade restrictions on their exports often retaliate with tariffs on imports into their own ports. The use of these trade regulations and barriers—a practice called **protectionism**—prevents the free flow of trade and drives up costs. Manufacturers have fewer markets in which to sell goods, and consumers have fewer choices in the marketplace.

Several agreements have been signed by countries around the world to settle some of these trade issues and to create more equitable

U.S. negotiators created the North American Free Trade Agreement (NAFTA) to increase trade with Canada and Mexico. But many U.S. citizens worried that if goods could be made and imported more cheaply from other countries, workers in the United States would lose their jobs. Here, protesters in California voice their opinions at a rally in 1993. NAFTA went into effect in 1994.

trade practices. The North American Free Trade Agreement (NAFTA), signed by Canada, the United States, and Mexico in 1993, is an example of such an agreement. One of the provisions of NAFTA eliminates tariffs on 10,000 different items over 15 years. Another provision allows one-half of all U.S. exports to enter Mexico duty-free (without charges to enter the country) within five years. Officials hope that NAFTA will create more trade with Mexico and eventually with the rest of Latin America. Officials plan for the trade agreement to extend to Central and South America by about 2005.

Promoting Growth ➤ The Port of Los Angeles is focusing on increasing the amount of trade with Pacific Rim nations, whose economies are rapidly growing. Years ago the port generated international business simply by advertising in foreign newspapers. Amid rapidly expanding global competition, the port's marketing department must do much more. In fact, the Port of Los Angeles has three main programs to promote growth in international trade.

The first program maintains 17 separate offices outside of the United States, many of them in Pacific Rim countries. In the mid-1990s, for example, the port opened offices in Vietnam and in China. Port representatives who work directly with foreign businessowners staff each office. The port representatives not only bring information about port facilities and services to foreign businessowners. The staff also helps foreign manufacturers find markets for their products in the United States. At the same time, the port representatives are trying to attract new markets for U.S. products in the host country. This method of face-to-face marketing has proved highly successful.

Another plan that increases international trade for the Port of Los Angeles is the Sister Port Program. The goals of the program are to exchange ideas, technology, and experience with other port cities to improve trade relations. The Port of Los Angeles's sister ports include Tokyo, Yokosuka, and Nagoya (Japan); Pusan (South Korea); Huang Pu (China); and Keelung (Taiwan). The sister ports are selected based on features they share with the Port of Los Angeles, such as location near a large urban area, large volumes of container traffic, and ongoing land reclamation projects like the Pier 300/400 Implementation Program. Each year the sister ports exchange five or six employees, who meet with various tenants (businesses located at the port) and with port personnel to

➤ The port does 47 percent of its international trade with Japan, 19 percent with South Korea, 15 percent with Taiwan, 6 percent with Hong Kong, 2 percent with China. All other countries make up 11 percent.

➤ Official estimates indicate that the volume of imports and exports moving through the Port of Los Angeles to and from the Pacific Rim will double in the next 25 years.

➤ The Pier 300/400 Implementation Program is the largest capital improvement program ever undertaken by any port in the United States.

The southern coast of South Korea is home to the port in Pusan, one of the sister ports to the Port of Los Angeles.

research the sister port. The employees on this exchange program take back to their home port a better understanding of how their work relates to the global shipping industry. Participants also gain a new network of personal contacts that can aid both ports and can create more business opportunities.

The third program is the establishment of a **foreign trade zone.** In 1994 the Port of Los Angeles applied for and received a foreign-trade-zone (FTZ) grant. Foreign and domestic merchandise may enter an FTZ zone for storage, assembly, exhibition, manufacture, and other processing without payment of customs duties or excise taxes. Almost all facilities at the Port of Los Angeles are included in FTZ No. 202. FTZ products are attractive to buyers because they are less expensive.

After an FTZ site is approved, each potential FTZ facility must submit an application to the local U.S. Customs Service for approval to

The California Cartage Company operates one of the port's foreign trade zone (FTZ) facilities. A worker inspects shoes (inset) *before they go to U.S. markets.*

operate. Two tenants on port property, Crescent Warehouse and California Cartage Company, have received approval to operate as FTZ facilities.

One of the commodities handled by California Cartage Company is copper mined in Arizona. The quantity of ore being handled and shipped by California Cartage has increased since getting FTZ approval, because the copper is cheaper for buyers to purchase.

As an FTZ operator, the company automatically became a member of the London Metal Exchange, which is a worldwide trade market for aluminum, copper, zinc, and silver. Manufacturers who buy these metals choose to deal with suppliers that have FTZ designation so they can purchase the ore at the lowest cost on the exchange. Then the buyer can store the ore in an FTZ without having to pay additional taxes or costs until the ore is needed for manufacturing or can be sold to another buyer. Most of the copper handled by California Cartage is eventually sold to Pacific Rim countries.

Global Energy Supplies and the Port ➤ Because of an international oil embargo (blockade) during the late 1970s, many countries without domestic oil supplies had to look for alternative energy sources. Japan and other Pacific Rim countries, for example, began to convert from oil to coal. This decision was met with enthusiasm by the United States, which contains 28 percent of the world's coal reserves. Coal has since become a valuable export and is helping to offset the U.S. trade deficit with Japan.

A system of conveyor belts loads mounds of coal (above) *onto ships. One of the GATX facilities* (right) *Is devoted to the export of coal and coke. A substance used for fuel, coke comes from the residue of carbonized coal.*

EXPORTING ENERGY TO JAPAN

Each year the Port of Los Angeles exports about 3.5 million tons of coal and petroleum coke. (Petroleum coke comes from the leftover residues of crude oil. The residual oil is pumped into a furnace, heated to a high temperature, and stored in drums.) The demand for coal in Japan, Taiwan, and other Asian nations is expected to rise to 192 million tons a year by the year 2005.

The coal is transported on railcars from mines in the western United States to the Port of Los Angeles. At Kaiser International Corporation's dry bulk terminal, coal is unloaded by rotary car dumping and is transferred onto conveyor belts, which load it directly onto ships for export or to a rail-mounted stacker for storage. The terminal can stockpile about 190,000 tons of coal, petroleum coke, and other dry-bulk commodities. The conveyor-feed shiploader moves 1,400 tons of coal an hour.

Once loaded with the coal, ships sail for Asian countries, where electricity plants burn the coal to make steam. The steam pushes turbines that produce electricity for power plants and industries.

Another valuable export is petroleum coke, a dry-bulk byproduct. With six oil refineries near the port, petroleum coke is readily available. Some coke comes to the port by truck or train from refineries in Wyoming. Like coal, the coke is loaded onto a ship and transported to Japan and other Asian destinations.

The Japanese use coke in their steel refineries to strengthen steel. The steel then is used in manufacturing automobiles. Within a few months, Japanese automobiles are loaded aboard carriers and shipped to the Port of Los Angeles. The port's export products thus return as manufactured imports, completing a supplier-consumer cycle.

Construction was begun in 1994 on the Los Angeles Export Facility.

So committed is Japan to buying more U.S. coal and petroleum coke, that Japanese coal companies, banks, and shipping lines have invested heavily in the new Los Angeles Export Facility, which is part of the Pier 300/400 Implementation Program. This new 120-acre dry-bulk terminal will have water depths of 72 feet, convenient storage facilities, rail access, enclosed cargo conveyor belts, and other features to attract bulk shippers.

The export facility also takes advantage of the port's location—near coal mines and refineries in Arizona, New Mexico, Colorado, and Utah. The easy access allows more coal to be exported to Japan. This partnership benefits both the United States and Japan and is an example of how trade and compatible goals can work to strengthen the ties between countries.

A port worker loads a container with a forklift. The port employs thousands of skilled laborers who specialize in various port operations.

More than 3,000 workers at the port belong to the International Longshoremen's & Warehousemen's Union. They work as stevedores, marine clerks, warehouse personnel, crane operators, and forklift drivers. The union has represented workers in the harbor since 1941.

◄ **The Port's Workforce**

The Los Angeles Police Department is responsible for serving all areas of the city including the port. To create a safe environment and to reassure foreign customers, however, the Port of Los Angeles maintains its own Port Police. It is the only port in the United States that has this additional protection.

More than 50 officers in the Port Police protect the Port of Los Angeles 24 hours a day.

They patrol the waterfront by boat, helicopter, automobile, and bicycle. The Port Police ensure safe boating within the harbor and monitor all hazardous materials. They participate in dive-and-rescue operations. One of their most important responsibilities is safeguarding the cargo at the port, estimated at a value of $74 billion a year. Cargo security and protection give tenants and customers the confidence that will keep them doing business with the Port of Los Angeles.

From mudflats and marshes to a worldwide commercial hub, the port has made valuable contributions to Los Angeles, southern California, the United States, and the world. The Port of Los Angeles is ready for the challenges and changes of the twenty-first century.

The Port Police patrols the harbor waters.

CITY OF ANGELS

The Port of Los Angeles is part of the huge city of Los Angeles. Los Angeles is the second most populous city in the United States, with more than 3.5 million people. The city and its surrounding metropolitan area have an even larger population of 14 million people. This metropolis sprawls across 4,083 square miles, making it larger than the combined area of the states of Delaware and Rhode Island.

Los Angeles is not a traditional city, with a concentrated urban center and distinct outer limits. Rather it is a collection of intermingling communities. Neighborhoods spread in all directions, encompassing hillside homes, small business districts, seaside resorts, and desert foothills. Commercial businesses, industrial

Towering office buildings overlook the tangle of Los Angeles's freeways.

63

Hollywood (above) *and Beverly Hills* (below) *are glitzy and famous Los Angeles suburbs.*

factories, and residential complexes are found in every area. One writer describes Los Angeles as a "patchwork of communities sewn into an ever-expanding quilt." Another refers to it as "a hundred suburbs in search of a city." Some communities within Los Angeles still have well-known identities. Hollywood, eight miles northwest of downtown Los Angeles, is one example. Other cities, like Beverly Hills, were never integrated and remain separate from Los Angeles. Beverly Hills is entirely surrounded by the city of Los Angeles.

From the downtown area encircling the original founding plaza and the Civic Center, metropolitan Los Angeles stretches 60 miles in all directions. Some of the far-reaching communities and districts—such as Studio City and Universal City—are in the San Fernando Valley. These communities are separated from downtown Los Angeles by mountains.

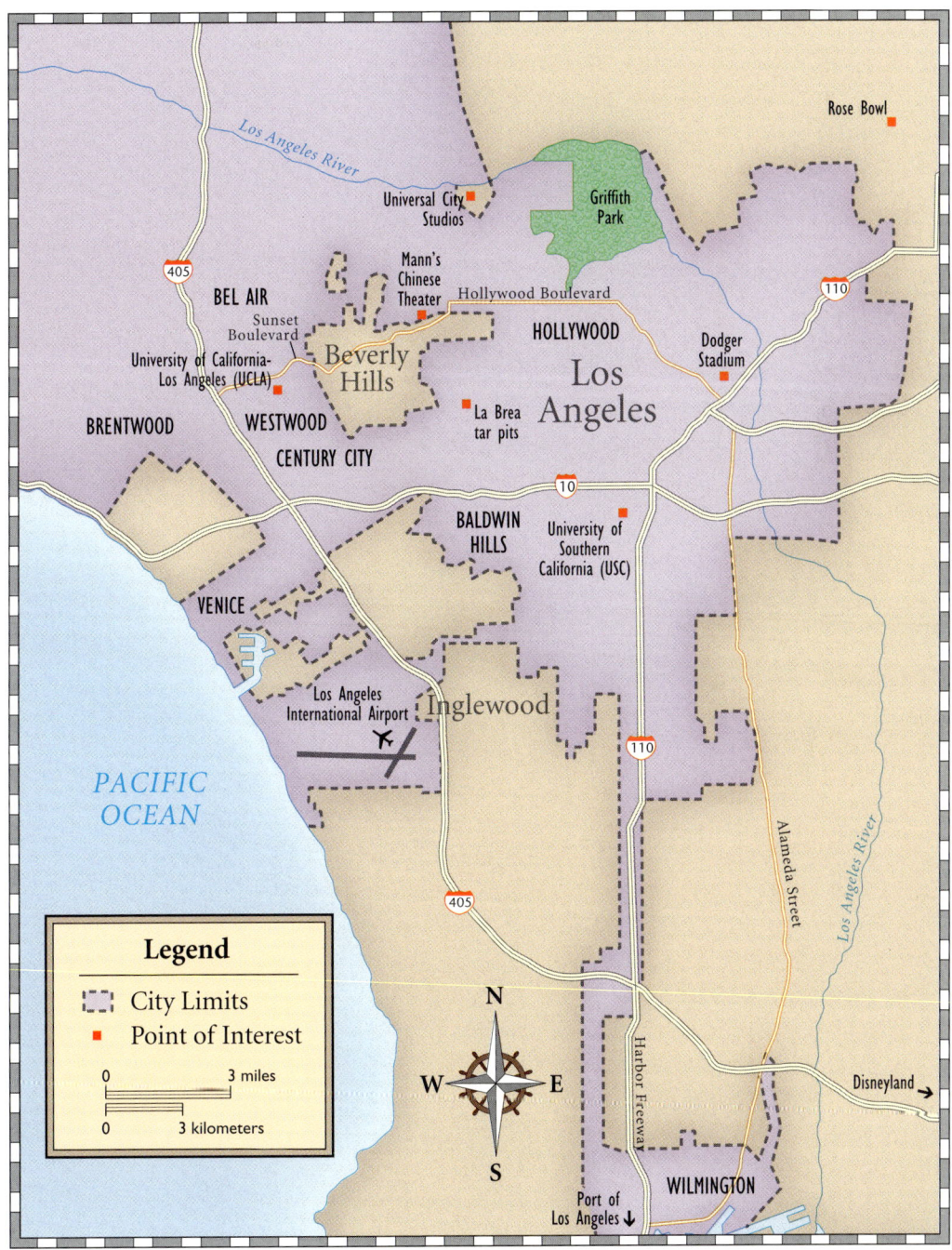

Los Angeles River

Rose Bowl

Universal City
Studios

Griffith
Park

Mann's
Chinese
Theater

Hollywood Boulevard

BEL AIR

HOLLYWOOD

Sunset
Boulevard

Beverly
Hills

Los
Angeles

Dodger
Stadium

University of California-
Los Angeles (UCLA)

La Brea
tar pits

BRENTWOOD

WESTWOOD

CENTURY CITY

BALDWIN
HILLS

University of
Southern
California (USC)

10

VENICE

Los Angeles
International Airport

Inglewood

PACIFIC
OCEAN

110

405

Alameda Street

Los Angeles River

Legend

City Limits

Point of Interest

0   3 miles

0   3 kilometers

N

W   E

S

Harbor Freeway

Disneyland →

WILMINGTON

Port of
Los Angeles ↓

405

110

405

Some residents live in the mountains and others live near the ocean. Los Angeles has 74 miles of seacoast. Malibu Beach, Venice, and Marina del Rey are some of the popular beach communities that draw thousands of tourists each year.

Beachcombers and sunbathers dot the sands of El Matador State Beach near Malibu.

Each area of Los Angeles has defining characteristics. Century City, between Beverly Hills and Westwood, is known for its many hotels. The University of California at Los Angeles is also in Westwood. The University of Southern California is in south central Los Angeles. The Fairfax area is home to the Farmer's Market and CBS Studios. Melrose has eclectic shops and art galleries. Pacific Palisades, Bel Air Estates, and Brentwood have large residential neighborhoods built on hills. Chinatown, Little Tokyo, and Koreatown are some of the ethnic neighborhoods in Los Angeles, although people of all

Los Angeles has a large Chinese population. In Chinatown visitors can find authentic Chinese cuisine, clothing, art, household goods, and more.

nationalities live throughout the metropolitan area.

A Diverse City ➤ Los Angeles has always had a diverse population. Since early times, people have immigrated to the city from all over the world. During the mid-1950s, when fishing and canning became major industries, many multiethnic communities sprang up in Los Angeles. Italian, Portuguese, Scandinavian, and Japanese fishing crews and their families settled in the area.

Latinos—people from Mexico, Central America, and South America—account for 40 percent of Los Angeles's population and make up the largest ethnic group in the city. African Americans comprise 14 percent of the population, and Asian Americans make up 10 percent. The rest of the population of Los Angeles is a multiethnic mixture, with Anglo-Americans constituting a little over 50 percent. So diverse is the population that 90 languages other than English are spoken by students in the city's public schools. Los Angeles has some of the largest Korean, Salvadoran, Filipino, Vietnamese, Chinese, Mexican, and Arab immigrant communities in the world. Each week brings different cultural events and celebrations to the city, as residents keep alive the traditions of their native lands.

All of these diverse communities and neighborhoods are connected by the largest freeway complex in the world. Freeways crisscross the

◀ **An Economic Giant**

The sprawling city of Los Angeles has experienced phenomenal economic and physical growth in the twentieth century.

landscape, providing access for motorists to all parts of the city. Vehicles can easily reach the Port of Los Angeles, making it convenient for manufacturers and businessowners throughout the city and southern California.

More than one-fourth of the workers in Los Angeles have jobs in the service sector, which includes banking, tourism, health care, legal aid, and education. Other leading service employers are in the wholesale and retail trade and in government.

Tourism provides service jobs in hotels, in restaurants, in theme parks, and at cultural attractions. Within minutes of the Los Angeles Harbor are world-class hotels, restaurants, museums, and a multitude of sports facilities. In the mid-1990s, more than 22 million tourists visited the area each year. About 76 percent of the visitors came from cities in the United States. The other 24 percent—roughly 5.3 million people—were international travelers.

Los Angeles is a leading manufacturing center for electronic equipment, clothing, processed foods, metal goods, chemicals, and printed materials. Manufacturing employs about 10 percent of the Los Angeles workforce. The aerospace industry, the city's largest, produces aircraft, spacecraft, and related equipment. Many large, well-known corporations also have their headquarters here. The city also has a major fresh-cut flower industry.

Los Angeles is probably best known as the Entertainment Capital of the World. Production crews film major movies and television shows in studios, at the city's beaches, near its mountains, and within its neighborhoods. The

The movie and television industries in Los Angeles are well known worldwide. A beach in Malibu provides the perfect backdrop for actors and film crews.

port is often the setting for a movie scene or a TV show. In addition to motion pictures and television broadcasting, the city is also home to the radio and music recording industries.

Along with tourism, the Port of Los Angeles is very important to the economy of Los Angeles. In southern California alone, the port and its industries create jobs for 247,000 people. How does this happen?

Employment increases by a ripple effect, similar to a rock being thrown into a pond. As more ships dock at the harbor, more port pilots are needed to steer the vessels. More longshoremen and stevedores are needed to unload the increasing amount of cargo. This increase requires more crane operators and forklift drivers, as well as accountants to handle payroll and book-

The Port's Contribution to the Economy

► The Port of Los Angeles creates 1 out of every 27 jobs in southern California.

► Los Angeles is the farthest of any major city from its harbor.

keeping. More cargo means trucking companies will hire additional drivers to carry shipments to the nearby rail yards. The trucks require fuel, a demand that requires more service stations and mechanics to keep the trucks rolling.

At the rail yards, more workers will be needed to unload cargo from trucks and load it onto trains. At its final destination, the cargo is unloaded and delivered to stores and warehouses, where employees sell the goods to consumers or use the imported items to manufacture new products. The more cargo and customers the port generates, the more the economy grows.

The port's economic impact affects not only the Los Angeles area, but the nation as a whole, generating employment for more than one million Americans. For example, the World Cruise Center continues to expand its services. By the late 1990s, the center will account for nearly 9,350 full-time jobs in Los Angeles and more than 585,000 jobs throughout the United

The Port of Los Angeles has the nation's fourth busiest cruise ship dock. In 1995 nearly 225,000 passengers passed through the World Cruise Center. The travel business creates thousands of jobs in the Los Angeles area and beyond.

States. Many of these jobs are directly related to the cruise industry—including positions with travel agencies, marketing firms, and advertising agencies. Companies supply cruise ships with food, linens, furniture, and products as basic as soap and cleaning supplies. Other jobs are created in the clothing industry for producing cruisewear sold onboard the ships and in department stores around the country.

Passengers from all over the world book cruises on liners based in the port. Before boarding their ships, they fly to Los Angeles, creating a need for more airport personnel, taxi and bus drivers, and hotel workers. It's easy to understand why the port must continually upgrade and expand services to attract new customers.

The Pier 300/400 Implementation Program also created jobs. Engineers, architects, construction workers, electricians, and many others teamed up on the project. The dredging phase alone generated 4,200 jobs. Construction of the Alameda Corridor established the need for about 10,000 workers. When the total expansion project is complete, estimates indicate that an additional 700,000 jobs will be generated in the Los Angeles region, and an additional 2.2 million jobs will be created throughout the nation.

Part of the port's steady growth is attributed to the large consumer base in the Los Angeles area. About 50 percent of all cargo imported through the port remains in the region. To have such a large consumer population in a port city is a tremendous incentive to foreign businessowners. When products are sold at a port of entry rather than shipped to other locations, manufacturers and distributors save a lot of money on transportation and storage and earn bigger profits.

Local Landmarks ➤ Some of the most well-known places in Los Angeles are within Hollywood. Along Hollywood Boulevard is the Walk of Fame, a long sidewalk featuring a row of stars, each of which honors a famous Hollywood actor. Mann's Chinese Theatre, an elaborately decorated movie theater on the Walk of Fame route, is known for the footprints, handprints, and engraved signatures of movie stars decorating the front court. Just northeast of the heart of Hollywood is the famous HOLLYWOOD sign on the side of a hill.

South of Hollywood is Hancock Park, which houses the Los Angeles County Museum of Art and the George C. Page Museum. The park is also the site of La Brea tar pits, a prehistoric graveyard full of the fossils of saber-toothed tigers, giant sloths, and other prehistoric creatures. The Page Museum displays many of the skeletons that scientists have dug up from the sticky asphalt bog. Griffith Park lies north of Hollywood. The 4,000-acre park is home to the

Mann's Chinese Theater (above) *in Hollywood is famous for its sidewalk. Many celebrities have left their handprints, footprints, and signatures* (right) *in the cement sidewalk.*

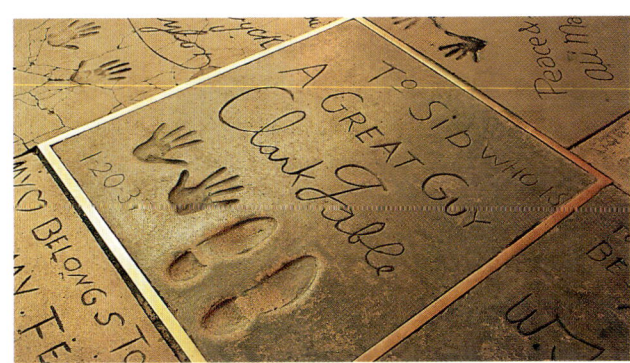

73

Griffith Observatory, the Autry Museum of Western Heritage, and the Los Angeles Zoo.

Downtown Los Angeles features City Hall, one of many buildings that make up the huge Civic Center complex. North of the complex is the Pueblo de Los Angeles, the site where 11 families from Mexico settled in 1781. Developers have restored the area to look like an old Mexican village. Dodger Stadium, where the Los Angeles Dodgers play baseball, lies just north of downtown.

Some of the most famous landmarks of Los Angeles are located in suburbs of the city. Disneyland, for example, is in Anaheim, about 20 miles southeast from downtown Los Angeles. Knott's Berry Farm, another popular attraction, is in Buena Park, which borders Anaheim on the west. In Pasadena, a northeastern suburb of Los Angeles, is the Rose Bowl. Every New Year's Day the Tournament of Roses Parade is followed by the Rose Bowl game, which features two of the nation's leading college football teams.

Off the Los Angeles coast lies Santa Catalina Island, one of the area's most popular destinations. Ferries from the Port of Los Angeles carry visitors to the island in about an hour. Much of

An artfully decorated float—made almost entirely of flower petals—cruises down the street during the Tournament of Roses Parade held every January.

A fireboat display leads a cruise ship through the Anderson Ship Channel. The port, although physically separated from the city of Los Angeles, is an integral part of the local economy.

➤ The Angel's Flight—a historic railroad—carries passengers up a steep, 315-foot climb from lower to upper downtown.

➤ Los Angeles is home to a number of professional and college sports teams. The Los Angeles Dodgers and the California Angels play baseball. Football fans root for the UCLA Bruins and the USC Trojans. The Los Angeles Lakers and the Los Angeles Clippers dunk basketballs. Hockey enthusiasts follow the Los Angeles Kings and the Anaheim Mighty Ducks.

Santa Catalina is wild and uninhabited, and very few cars can be found. People get around on bicycles, on foot, or on golf carts. Besides kayaking, parasailing, and jet skiing, funseekers explore the island's Underwater Park, an off-shore area of kelp beds and colorful wildlife reserved for scuba divers and snorkelers.

Back at the port, visitors tour the SS *Lane Victory*—a World War II cargo ship open to tourists. Shops, restaurants, museums, and beaches also attract many people to the port. Although the Port of Los Angeles lies outside the heart of the city, it is an integral part of the city's economy and culture. In the future, the port will continue to grow and develop, facilitating trade between one of the largest U.S. cities and the growing economies of Pacific Rim nations.

GLOSSARY

breakbulk cargo: A term used to refer to noncontainerized general cargo. This cargo category includes items packaged in separate units, such as boxes, cases, and pallets, as well as heavy machinery that is too big to be transported in a container.

bulk cargo: Raw products, such as grains and minerals, that are not packaged in separate units. Dry bulk cargo is typically piled loosely in a ship's cargo holds, while liquid bulk cargo is piped into a vessel's storage tanks.

containerization: A shipping method in which a large amount of goods is packed in standardized **containers.**

dredging: The process of digging up and removing soil from the bed of a lake or river bottom. Dredging deepens the waterway and creates a stockpile of soil that can be used as landfill elsewhere.

dry dock: A dock where a vessel is kept out of the water so that repairs can be made to the parts that lie below the water line.

foreign (or free) trade zone: An area near a transportation hub such as a seaport or an airport where goods can be imported without paying tariffs or other import taxes. Foreign traders may store, display, assemble, or process goods in these zones before shipping them to the place where they will eventually be sold. Approximately 70 free trade zones are in operation throughout the United States.

gantry crane: A crane mounted on a platform supported by a framed structure that runs on parallel tracks so as to span or rise above a ship for purposes of loading and unloading heavy cargo.

hopper car: A freight car with a floor that slants downward toward a hinged door, which swings open to release bulk cargo.

intermodal transportation: A system of transportation in which goods are moved from one type of vehicle to another, such as from a ship to a train or from a train to a truck, in the course of a single trip.

mitigation credit: A type of credit awarded to an organization for restoring an endangered ecosystem. Accumulated credits are needed for permission from the U.S. government to build or expand industrial developments that impact the environment.

protectionism: A trade philosophy of protecting a nation's economy by controlling trade with other countries. Countries that protect their markets often allow in only certain types of goods.

TEU: Twenty-foot equivalent unit. Container traffic is measured in TEUs. One TEU represents a container that is 20 feet long, 8 feet wide, and 8.5 feet or 9.5 feet high.

PRONUNCIATION GUIDE

Bahía de los Fumos	bah-EE-ah day lohs FOO-mohs
Cabrillo, Juan Rodriguez	kah-BREE-yoh, WAHN rod-REE-gays
Cerritos	say-REE-tohs
El Pueblo de Nuestra Señora la Reina de Los Ángeles	ehl PWEH-bloh day noo-AYS-trah say-NYOH-rah lah RAY-nah day lohs AHN-heh-lehs
Huang Pu	WAHNG POO
Pusan	POO-sahn
Sepulveda, Diego	say-pool-VAY-dah, dee-AY-goh
Yokosuka	yoh-KOH-suh-kuh

INDEX

METRIC CONVERSION CHART

WHEN YOU KNOW	MULTIPLY BY	TO FIND
inches	2.54	centimeters
feet	0.3048	meters
miles	1.609	kilometers
square feet	0.0929	square meters
square miles	2.59	square kilometers
acres	0.4047	hectares
pounds	0.454	kilograms
tons	0.9072	metric tons
bushels	0.0352	cubic meters
gallons	3.7854	liters

ABOUT THE AUTHOR

Dianne MacMillan, a former elementary-school teacher, is an accomplished author who has published both fiction and nonfiction children's books. She also pens articles for juvenile magazines and regularly visits classrooms to talk with young people about her writing experiences. She has written *Missions of the Los Angeles Area,* a Lerner title, and *Elephants,* under the Carolrhoda imprint. MacMillan has three daughters and lives with her husband in Orange Park Acres, California.

ACKNOWLEDGMENTS

I would like to thank the many people at the Port of Los Angeles who gave me assistance. In particular I am grateful to Donald W. Rice, Director of Environmental Management; Ralph G. Appy, Assistant Director of Environmental Management; and Barbara Yamamoto in Public Affairs who generously provided contacts and information.